WILD WOLF CLAIMING

A HOWLS WEREWOLF ROMANCE

GRACE GOODWIN

Wild Wolf Claiming: Copyright © 2016
by Grace Goodwin
ISBN: 978-1-7959-0175-8
Interstellar Brides® is a registered trademark
of KSA Publishing Consultants Inc.
All Rights Reserved. No part of this book may be reproduced or transmitted in any form or by any means, electrical, digital or mechanical including but not limited to photocopying, recording, scanning or by any type of data storage and retrieval system without express, written permission from the author.

Published by KSA Publishers
Goodwin, Grace
Wild Wolf Claiming, Howls Werewolf Romance

Cover Copyright © 2017 by Grace Goodwin
Cover Photo © canstock: arturkurjan; GraphicStock

Publisher's Note:
This book was written for an adult audience. The book may contain explicit sexual content. Sexual activities included in this book are strictly fantasies intended for adults and any activities or risks taken by fictional characters within the story are neither endorsed nor encouraged by the author or publisher.

INTERSTELLAR BRIDES® PROGRAM

YOUR mate is out there. Take the test today and discover your perfect match. Are you ready for a sexy alien mate (or two)?

VOLUNTEER NOW!
interstellarbridesprogram.com

GET A FREE BOOK!

JOIN MY MAILING LIST TO BE THE FIRST TO KNOW OF NEW RELEASES, FREE BOOKS, SPECIAL PRICES AND OTHER AUTHOR GIVEAWAYS.

http://freescifiromance.com

CHAPTER 1

ily

My ears buzzed with that strange little ringing noise I got when I was being watched. It had me checking every mirror on the car and accelerating to ninety. Which was stupid. No one was here. Wherever *here* was. I was over a thousand miles from home in an unfamiliar car. Idaho was as far from East Springs, Tennessee as I could get before I hit the crowds on the west coast. That was out for me. Too many people. Too much water.

I never thought I'd ever run away from home, not at twenty-one. But that was exactly what I was doing. No, not running away from home, running away from *him*. Robert Nathanial Howard *the third.*

"Asshole." Reaching for the radio dial, I cranked up the volume to drown out my memories. Oh, he hadn't raped me, but he'd had a hard time listening when I told him no, to stop, that I didn't want it. He'd slowed down, pulled back, looked at me like I was lying. Said some bullshit about scenting my change, like I was a confused thirteen-year-old just hitting puberty.

Whatever. He hadn't seemed convinced until I'd said my grandfather would kill him. That had shut him down, wilted his dick and had him rolling off me faster than fleeing a fire.

Everyone in East Springs was afraid of my family, especially Grandad. Weirdly afraid. But I didn't ask too many questions. Grandad ran the town and that was just the way things were. That was the way things had always been. My mom was gone now, leaving me alone with him. We weren't touchy-feely huggers. Hell, he was a distant, cold old man with ice blue eyes and a temper I avoided rousing. *Everyone* avoided rousing.

Even worse, being around him reminded me of my mom, which hurt. Since I looked a lot like her, I figured he felt the same. After she died a couple years ago, well, Grandad and I pretty much avoided each other. But neither one of us had to look far to be reminded of my mother. All we had to do was look in the mirror and those ice blue eyes stared right back at us.

But Grandad was always there for me, whether I wanted him to be or not. He ran our town, thought he ran my life. Even now, a thousand miles away, he'd find a way to keep tabs on me. That was just what he did. So of course he heard about Robbie getting a little too pushy with me, and I hadn't told a soul.

People in East Springs paired off young. Too young, in my opinion. Most of the women were head over heels in lust by the time they were nineteen. That was insane. I had somehow avoided that. So far. Although if Robbie'd had his way, I'd have been paired off with him whether I wanted to be or not. I wasn't going to be with a guy just because he pushed himself on me.

Not that Robbie was a terrible human being. He was gorgeous, as men in my home town tended to be. Over six foot with chiseled features, muscles everywhere and eyes that looked right through me. But he wasn't for me. I didn't know what I wanted, but it definitely wasn't him.

Ever since my sixteenth birthday, I felt like I'd been watched, like the rest of my family was just waiting for a hormone bomb to drop inside me and turn me into a sex-crazed maniac like some of my younger cousins. Maybe that would have helped Robbie's chances. Maybe I would've been so horny it wouldn't matter so much who I was with.

I'd fooled around a bit, sure, but I'd never felt the lust, the need, my friends had mentioned. Because of this, I figured maybe there was something wrong with me. I liked hooking up just fine, it just wasn't worth obsessing over. With Robbie I'd tried, really tried, but his tongue had all but made me gag when he shoved it in my mouth and his hands on my bare skin had made my skin crawl. And look what that got me?

"A black eye and a bad attitude." I checked the damage I'd inflicted in the rear view mirror. The fading green and yellow bruising was almost completely gone now. And the light coating of makeup I wore hid the rest. I'd been stupid, running blindly in the dark. The doctor had said I was lucky I hadn't lost an eye. Robbie had been skulking around, oozing fury. And yeah, it was obvious the doctor didn't believe I'd done it to myself. He'd thought Robbie hit me and I was covering for my boyfriend.

As if. But it *had* felt good to make Robbie suffer.

Besides, a little makeup and I still looked good, especially since I'd left the jerk two time zones away. The sun had pinked my cheeks. My eyes were sparkling with something other than rage, and I felt free. Happy.

If I'd done what I wanted to do when Robbie was feeling me up, I'd be sitting in a jail cell right now. Fortunately, I was very, very good at controlling my temper. My mother had drilled that into me since I could walk. *A Windbourn never loses their temper.*

There were a lot of rules like that. Don't lose your temper. Don't draw attention to yourself in public. Don't run too fast. No sports. Don't. Don't.

"Don't date a member of the Howard family," I added. I'd broken that one, and look how fantastically that little adventure played out.

They were a wealthy family that lived farther north. The Howard family pretty much owned the small town they lived in, just like the Winterbourns ran East Springs. And the rivalry between the Howards and the Windbourns went as far back as I could remember. No, much longer than my lifetime. Our high school hated theirs, our mayor hated theirs. It was intense and very small town. And me with Robbie? It had seemed very Romeo and Juliet…well, without the Romeo and Juliet. I'd seen to that. I'd found the entire thing ridiculous.

Sure, he was hot. Rippling muscles, dark hair, the face of a god. He'd said all the right things, done all the right things. Until he got me beneath him. Then something inside me had come roaring to life, but not with desire.

I'd never felt anything like it, before or since. And frankly, the ferocity of my reaction scared the shit out of me.

I'd wanted to kill him. And not in a pretty way, in a gouge out his eyes and rip his throat out kind of way.

A huge overreaction for a guy I'd *invited* into my bed. I'd done it partly to test myself because I was tired of having the reputation of being a frigid witch, and partly to defy my Grandad and his legion of spies that were always following me around since my mom died, watching me like I was a ticking time bomb.

I wanted to want Robbie. I had. I'd tried, but there just

hadn't been anything *right* about it. I wanted my heart to race. I wanted to feel wild and desperate and out of control. I wanted passion like all my friends spoke about, that I knew existed with the right guy. I'd wanted to feel that and I'd hoped Robbie would be it. It would've been so simple.

Meh. He'd been fine. Fooling around had been fine. *Fine.* But the whole time I'd been thinking about my college application to Lewiston and Cooke College, wondering if they'd take me, wondering if my father's cousins still lived in the same small town in Idaho. Robbie had been touching me, kissing me, his body hot and hard and pressing me into the bed and I'd been wondering how I'd done on the math placement exam.

Which was just messed up.

A rabbit darted into the road and seeing my approach, scurried back into the thick woods that were right up on the road's edge, bringing me back from my thoughts. Fine. I didn't want fine. I wanted more. I wanted *everything*. Sweaty skin, ragged breathing, heated touches, soft caresses, whispered words. Blinding pleasure. It was out there, with someone. I put my fingers to my almost healed cheek. Just not with Robbie and not in East Springs.

My spine tingled and my skin broke out with goose bumps despite the heat of the sun shining through the trees. I had the top down and my dark hair flying wild behind me. The sun was baking my skin, but a chill moved through me and I thought I saw a shadow racing beside me in the woods just off the highway.

But that was freaking impossible. Right? Nothing could run that fast.

Scared now, and feeling stupid about it, I slowed the car down to sixty-five, relieved when I saw a sign for Black Falls. Five miles. Which meant about five minutes until I could get out of this car, stretch my legs, get checked in to a hotel and take a nice, hot shower.

Thump. Thump. Thump.

"What the hell?" The steering wheel jerked in my hands and I had to hold on tightly to keep the car from swerving off the road, right into the forest.

Foot off the gas, I eased to the side, fighting the car the whole way. When I finally rolled to a stop, I took a second to catch my breath, let my heart rate slow. Muttering a string of curses, I got out and walked around.

The right front tire was flat as a pancake and I hadn't seen another car for a solid ten minutes. I was out in the middle of Nowhereville.

"Damn it, damn it, damn it!" I was so not in the mood for this. Sure, I could change a damn tire, but I was wearing a bright pink sundress and my brand new white sandals. I had a mani-pedi in hot pink to match, and I didn't want to drive into my new town, to a new school and a new life with tire grease and dirt all over me.

Hands on my hips, I scanned the road in both directions. Nothing.

Bending over the passenger side door, I grabbed my cell phone from the cup holder.

Nope. Zero bars. I looked around at the trees. The never-ending trees. No bars meant I couldn't splurge for a tow truck even if I wanted to.

And my spare was buried in the trunk under just about everything I owned.

Tossing the phone on the passenger seat, I spun and leaned my backside against the car door. "This is not happening."

I would not cry. Wouldn't do it.

A Windbourn never shows weakness in public. Don't cry, dear. Never, ever cry where they can see you.

Holy hell. How many times had I heard my mother say that one?

Evidently enough, because the sting of tears dried up instantly. With a sigh, I walked around, pulled the keys out of the ignition and opened the trunk. If I had to unpack the whole damn car, I might was well get started.

"Need some help?"

The voice was deep, masculine and raced through me like an electric current. I jumped, hitting my head on the open trunk before slowly pivoting on my heel to find the sexiest man I'd ever seen.

He was six-three if he was an inch, with golden brown hair and amber eyes that were watching me with laser focus. He wasn't ogling, but looking me straight in the eye. Somehow, that didn't mean much. I had the feeling he was acutely aware of every inch of me without even shifting his gaze.

"I...um, I have a flat." I tried to peek around him, but I didn't see a car or a truck or a motorcycle. What had he done? Run out here? "Where's your car?"

He laughed and I found myself smiling back. He tucked his hands into his jeans pockets, his stance casual. "There's a fishing hole just over that ridge." He angled his chin behind him. "I heard your radio, and then the tire blow. Thought you might need some help."

Oh. Damn. He'd heard me blaring Taylor Swift? I felt my cheeks turning pink, but there wasn't anything I could do about it. And my mother had never told me any Windbourn rules about music.

"I can change the tire for you. Or I can call my cousin, Drake, and he can come out and give you a tow."

"There's no cell service," I blurted out.

His lithe, well-muscled frame was defined by a pair of well-worn, well shaped jeans. They cupped his hips and butt, and his...ahem, quite large package. Realizing I was the one who was ogling, I jerked my gaze up to his flat stomach, broad chest and even broader shoulders. A simple black t-shirt shouldn't look so good. Neither should his corded arms and big hands.

Big hands meant—

"So, got a tire iron then?" he asked.

I whipped my gaze up to his, saw the slight turn at the corner of his full lips. Yeah, he'd caught me looking and my cheeks had to be the same pink as my dress.

When I tilted my head, unsure, he stepped forward and held out his hand. For the briefest of moments, I could have sworn I saw his amber eyes turn dark brown. "I'm Kade."

I knew I shouldn't, but I wanted to feel his skin. Wanted to see how big his hand was in comparison to mine. I wanted him to touch me, wondered if I'd actually feel small and feminine. Somehow protected. I placed my hand in his and it was like my entire body came roaring to life.

That hormones bomb that everyone had been waiting to go off?

Boom.

"Lily…Lily Windbourn."

CHAPTER 2

ade

FUCK. Me. A Windbourn? Here? In Black Falls territory?

No wonder I'd been drawn to her, compelled to shadow a car driving along the edge of national forest. I'd scented her easily, and no wonder. She was in a damn convertible. Peaches and vanilla shampoo and something else that I couldn't define, something that was uniquely *her*.

Long, dark hair hung down her back, tousled and ruffled by the wind. Her cheeks were sun kissed, her lips full and I wanted to kiss them. And her eyes. Fuck, her eyes were so pale, so vivid. I saw worry and curiosity combined. The interest was there, but without her scent, without picking up the new tang of arousal, I wouldn't know for sure. Her wolf certainly wasn't presenting itself. No, if it had, she'd be bent over the hood of her car, her dress pushed up about her waist and my cock buried deep.

I wanted to howl. My wolf wanted her, even rose to the

surface for a moment. Hell, I wanted her. Wanted to touch and taste and listen to her whisper my name as I filled her with my….

Sure. Not going there, not with her. I had to hold a hand over my cock to hide my reaction to her. Lust. Instant heat. The urge to bite her, mark her, make her mine. That was the long and short of it. It was intense, powerful, the need to take her, the need to claim her roared through my head until I had a hard time concentrating on making small talk.

What the hell? Sure, I'd been attracted to women before, could smell their interest, but it hadn't been like this. No, I could practically taste Lily. My mouth watered to do just that. Her lips and lower. Her nipples, which were prominent beneath the thin fabric of her pink dress. And lower still, to the sweet apex of her thighs.

Yeah, I wanted to eat the pussy of a damn Windbourn. The Windbourns were the most powerful werewolf family in the east, hell, maybe in the world. What was she doing here? This was Black Falls territory. We controlled this area of the country. What the hell was her alpha thinking, sending her up here alone? Did she have permission to be here? Or would taking her into town stir up a hornet's nest of trouble?

That was a stupid question. Of course she'd stir up a shit ton of trouble. She smelled like heaven, powerful and sweet and ripe for the taking. Thankfully, I'd scented her first, found her first. Once other unmated males in the area picked up the sweet peaches and vanilla, I wouldn't be alone in my interest. Which meant I'd probably have to fight for the right to claim her in the moonlight, take care of her, see to her pleasure when her body suffered the almost violent lust of an awakening.

When even that thought didn't deter my wolf, I knew I was in trouble already. Damn it.

I couldn't touch her. Not here. Not now. Pack protocol

required claiming her in an official ceremony, where all other contenders were near her to offer their scent and protection. But from the sweet smell of her skin, and the interest she was throwing off with those ice blue eyes, I'd get my chance soon enough. Her wolf was quiet, but wouldn't remain so for long. I'd say it was close to her time. Real close, since just looking at me had brought her body to life. Judging by the scent rising from her, I'd say her panties were ruined. My wolf was pleased with that, for she was definitely responsive. And when her wolf came out? She was going to play with me and no one else. Claiming ceremony or not.

"Where are you headed?" I asked, trying to keep her eyes on my face and not on my throbbing cock. No doubt if she looked, she'd see the thick bulge beneath the worn denim.

"Black Falls. I start classes at Lewiston and Cooke next week."

My wolf settled, happy knowing she wasn't passing through. Prepared to wait for the right time to claim her. I'd never wanted to mark a woman before, and the urge was powerful, making my jaw clench, my canines ache. She'd be just a few miles away at school. I had time. I could watch over her, protect her from harm—and from other unmated wolves—until she was ready. Until I could make her mine.

Mine? Where the hell had that thought come from?

The wolf inside me chuckled and settled into a watchful stance. *Mine. Mine. Mine.* The werewolf in me had a simple mind, driven more by instinct than logic. And yes, he intended to claim her. He wanted her. No questions, no bullshit. That was the wolf way. I'd heard about it, had friends tell me what it was like to meet their mates, but now...

Mate? Had I just thought of her as my mate?

"Damn it."

"What?" She jumped at my outburst and I shook myself quickly to apologize.

"No. I'm sorry. That wasn't directed at you. Let's get that tired changed and you into town, Lily." I said her name for the first time and couldn't wait to say it again and again as I buried myself balls deep in her body and put my mark on her neck.

* * *

Lily, one week later

I FELT his hands on me, his lips, the rub of his thick cock against my leg. My back arched as kisses landed on my belly. Lower and lower until I parted my thighs. I did it, no coaxing needed. I wanted him there. I was wet and it was all for him. I wanted him to know I ached for him, that I was ready. I wanted that cock deep inside me, stretching me, filling me. I wanted him to come deep inside, to literally coat me in his seed. Mark me. Claim me. I wanted to smell like him.

"Yes," I murmured. "Please."

I wasn't beyond begging. I *needed* it.

It wasn't his cock that slid over my heated folds, but his tongue. He knew exactly what he was doing, exactly what I needed. And when he flicked my clit, I came. Just. Like. That.

"Yes!" I cried again, this time I opened my eyes, saw the dark dorm room. Felt the cool night air on my sweaty skin. Shook from the remnants of the orgasm that still hummed in my body. It wasn't a guy's head between my thighs, but my fingers. I was alone in my room, thank god, because I'd had the most intense sex dream.

My white nightgown was up about my waist, my thighs parted, sheets tangled. Yeah, if I'd gotten a roommate instead of a single, she'd think I was a sex starved nympho.

Well, I hadn't been until now. Until Black Falls. God, the

second I'd settled into my dorm, I'd turned into a horny mess. No, it hadn't been then. It had been the second Kade appeared on the side of the road. I'd been instantly attracted and even making myself come didn't ease the ache. It was only getting worse and I was going insane.

He'd come by every night, taken me to dinner, held doors and behaved like the perfect gentleman. But I didn't want chivalry at the moment, I wanted him to shove me up against a wall and fuck my brains out. No one had ever done that. Hell, I'd never wanted it before. But since meeting Kade? My nipples were always hard and my bras chafed the tender tips. My pussy was dripping like a damned faucet. I'd already ruined several pairs of panties. I was going crazy thinking every time a soft breeze came in through my open dorm window that I could smell him. I'd had to touch myself twice yesterday, locking the door, leaning against it and sticking my hand down my shorts.

And those hadn't been the first times. After Kade helped me carry my things up to my room and left with a quick smile and a heated gaze, I'd had to lift up my sundress and make myself come sitting on the side of my bed.

I wanted sex. I *needed* it. And every one of my fantasies had involved Kade. I thought maybe I was just losing my mind, but then I'd seen the other guys in my building and felt…nothing. Many of them eyed me the way Kade had, as if they wanted to gobble me right up.

The way I was behaving, I couldn't blame them. It was like they could sense how wild I was feeling, believed all they had to do was push me, just a little, and I'd be begging. God, it was like I had a bright neon sign on my forehead that said *I'm desperate, fuck me now.*

I pushed my nightgown back over my thighs, but my fingers were sticky with my juices. Groaning, I got up, grabbed a robe to go out into the hall and down the hallway to the bathroom. While I had a single, I was just like every other person on the floor sharing a communal bathroom.

I didn't turn on my light. I didn't need to. The light from the full moon offered a bright glow to my stark room. I also had keen eyesight and could see quite well in the dark, always could, since I was a little girl. Other little kids asked for night-lights and glowing toys. I put the covers over my head so I could huddle in the dark and actually fall asleep.

I opened the door to the hallway and gasped. Backlit by the industrial lighting stood Robbie.

"Hey Lily," he said. "Couldn't help but overhear you." He took a deep breath. Another. With a dark look in his eyes I'd never seen before, he leaned closer and nearly pressed his nose to my shoulder. A shiver raced over his skin when he straightened, as if he'd just been shocked with a jolt of electricity.

I took a slight step back. Was he *sniffing* me?

"Um." I didn't say more than that. He'd overheard what? Me crying out as I came in my sex dream? That was embarrassing. I avoided his gaze, but when he said nothing more, I looked up. His eyes. They weren't brown or blue or even green. No, they were gold. Like weirdly gold. "What are you doing here, Robbie? How did you find me?"

"Mr. Windbourn sent us after you, Lily. You should have told him you were leaving. It's dangerous."

That roused me from my embarrassment and I latched onto the rage flooding me with a sense of relief. Anything was better than feeling helpless and weak in front of him. "I'm a grown adult. I don't need permission to do anything."

He laughed, the sound harsh, one I'd never heard from him before and it made my nerves twist like pretzels until my entire body felt on the verge of an explosion. "You are so naïve, baby. Of course you need permission. The Benson brothers are waiting in the car. Pack your shit. You have ten minutes."

I dug my heels in and crossed my arms. I'd worked hard to get into this school. I filled out all their forms, took all their tests, handled all the financial aid on my own. No way I was going to tuck tail and go home just because Robbie was looming over me with a frown on his face and two of my Grandad's henchmen were in the car. "I'm not leaving."

His expression changed to one I did recognize, lust. "There is another option."

"What's that?"

"We finish what we started in your bedroom." He lifted a hand to my cheek, his thumb gently stroking the remnants of the bruise around my eye, and for the first time ever, my body heated at his touch. I still wanted to punch him, but I wanted to sleep with him, too. No, not sleep. My pussy throbbed, yet I knew I didn't like him, that I wasn't interested in him as a man, only as a…

As a what? I wasn't the kind of girl who did casual sex.

But maybe I was.

"Sorry about the doctor," I muttered, my guilt rising to the surface just like every other emotion I'd ever felt in my life appeared to be. I was a mess, my head spinning, my body totally out of control. All I wanted was someone to make it all go away, to touch me and make me come, then hold me and tell me it was all going to be okay.

"Nothing to be sorry about. Let me come in and I'll take care of you." His voice was calm and deep and gentle, as if he already knew he'd won. Maybe he had. My breasts were heavy, my heart racing. Something was wrong with me and his next words confirmed it. "You need to be touched, don't you? Filled? You need about a dozen more orgasms, baby and I can give them to you."

His finger traced my lower lip and it took a supreme act

of will not to flick my tongue out over the tip and taste him. I stepped back some more, put my hand on the knob. I was equally eager and repulsed by his offer. I didn't want *him*, but I definitely *wanted.*

I shook my head. I was not a stupid animal. I was not a stray dog in heat. If I was going to sleep with someone, it was *not* going to be Robbie from back home. Or the stupid Benson brothers. "No. Go away. Go home and tell Grandad to leave me alone."

Slamming the door shut, I flipped the deadbolt and backed away.

His sigh was loud, so loud in my ears that I winced. "I can't do that, Lily. You need me, need me to kiss you and touch you and make you mine." His hand must have been pressed flat to the door because I heard the slide of his palm on wood as he spoke, and imagined he was touching me instead. "You need me, baby. I've been waiting for this. It's time for us to be together. Let me in, I promise I'll make it good for you."

I did. I did need, but not him. I needed *someone,* and that scared the shit out of me. Why did I feel like I wanted to grab him with both hands, pull him into my room, tug up my nightgown and beg him to take me? Why did I want him to bend me over my bed and sink into me as hard and fast as he could?

Shit. There was something *really* wrong with me. Had I been drugged? My skin ached, literally ached with the need to be touched. I ran my hands up and down my arms, around my neck and into my hair in an effort to soothe myself. But it didn't work. Nothing worked.

Worse? My eyes ached, and even though I hadn't turned on the light, I could see everything in my room perfectly, which was normal. But now I could even read the small black print on the package labels on my favorite crackers across the room. I could smell the dirty laundry hidden behind closed closet doors, and the scent of the pine cleaner they'd used in the bathrooms down the hall. I knew without trying hard that the two students that lived across the hall had eaten pepperoni pizza with olives for dinner.

I could *smell* it, all of it.

CHAPTER 3

ily

"Lily?" Robbie knocked on the door once more, the sound so faint I shouldn't have been able to hear it, but I could. I could hear the blood rushing through my veins, the insects inside the walls? Little legs, millions of them, scrambling and moving with purpose.

"Lily? It's okay. I can hear your heart racing. Don't be scared. Just let me in. Everything will be all right, I promise."

No. It wasn't all right. I wasn't all right. And he wasn't going to go away. He wanted to get me naked and I wanted him to do it. That disturbed me more than anything.

I jumped when he tried the doorknob, ran around to the far side of my bed.

"Lily!" he shouted.

I went to the open window, looked out into the darkness. The moon lit up the trees, my side of the dorm backed up to a large open park, and beyond that was national forest. Being on the ground floor, I could see nothing beyond, but knew the forest stretched on for miles. Something was calling me to climb from the window, to go out into the night.

And then I saw the reason. A tall form, his white shirt almost blindingly bright under the light of the moon. I knew who it was, could see him as clearly as if it were broad daylight. My nipples ached and my clit throbbed as I took in his dark hair and full lips. He wore the same snug style jeans, but he looked wilder somehow, his hair sticking up as if he'd been running his fingers through it.

I wanted to run *my* fingers through it. No. Forget that. I just wanted him. All of him.

Kade.

If the choice was stay in my room and try to resist Robert's advances or do something completely insane? I knew what I had to do.

Putting my hands on the window frame, I shoved the screen out of my way, climbed through the wide opening, took a deep breath and jumped.

* * *

Kade

SHE CLIMBED OUT THE WINDOW, her white nightgown all but glowing as it billowed around her thighs. She was running to me, her pace swift, her gait smooth. I met her, wanted to touch, to kiss her, but she didn't stop, only tugged on my wrist.

"We have to go. Now."

I heard the frantic energy of her voice, scented her arousal. It was growing stronger which meant her time was upon her. I glanced back at her dorm, saw the silhouette of a figure standing in her window just before we cut into the woods.

"Who is he?"

"Later. I'll explain, I promise, but we have to go now!"

She was mine, and she was with me so I let it go...for now. We ran then, but I led. I knew the forest, knew it like the back of my hand. Knew where to go to keep her safe.

"We should shift." Escaping danger in wolf form was safer than in human. Did she not shift? Was she unable? A thought flicked through my brain. Did she even know she was a wolf?

Fuck, that meant—

"Shift what?"

When I didn't answer, she kept talking.

"He followed me," she said, her voice coming out in pants. I slowed to match her shorter gait. "He followed me all the way from home."

"Who is he?" It didn't really matter, only that it was someone she didn't want to see. Someone she was afraid of. That she was willing to climb out a window to escape.

"Robert. He followed me from Tennessee and brought two of my Grandad's goons. They drove all the way from East Springs."

A wolf—he had to be one—had followed her across the country? It wasn't much of a surprise. I'd picked up her scent in the woods earlier and it had called to me, all but pulled me to her again like a magnet. It would have been easy for the wolf to follow her, especially if he knew her well. "Two goons?"

She laughed but there was no joy in the sound. "Babysitters. That's one of the reasons I left." Her laugh turned to a sigh and she slowed to a stop. "It's one of the reasons I left home. Ever since my mom died, Grandad has these guys following me around all the time. I mean, yeah, I'm from a small town, but it's ridiculous. I'm not a three year old. I don't need a keeper."

But she did. She just didn't know it. Not that it mattered. Not anymore. She was mine now. Mine, and if the idiots who followed her tried to take her from me I'd rip out their throats and send them to Lily's grandfather special delivery.

"They're your grandfather's men?"

"Yes."

"All three of them?"

She bit her lip and looked away, a flush covering her cheeks. "I used to date one of them, but I don't want him." Her adorable frown turned confused and when I saw the confusion shift to fear, I pulled her into my arms and held her close, pressed her to me so her wolf would know I was here as she continued. "I never wanted him before. But I think something's wrong with me."

"There's nothing wrong with you." Running my hand up and down her back to soothe her, rage filled me as she melted into my arms. But holding her, being the one she came to felt perfect and so right. I'd been running on instinct until now, a lone wolf serving as enforcer for my alpha. Now? Nothing mattered but her, and everything inside me settled around that truth. She was like gravity. I didn't question her existence in my life, or her importance. She was just…mine.

How was it that she'd never been told what she was? True that some children didn't carry enough wolf blood to shift. Those people lived their lives unaware of their genetic history. But Lily was the granddaughter of the Windbourn alpha. The odds of her not becoming a full wolf were—well —next to none. She should have been told.

There would be no place safe for her to hide. The wolves chasing her would be able to scent her. And the one I'd seen in her window? He wanted her for himself. Hell, every unmated male wolf in Black Falls would be able to scent her. None could miss the ripe essence of her, ready to be claimed, fucked and mated.

My balls ached to have her, to make her mine.

Mate, my wolf howled.

Yeah, no one would get her but me. But there was only one way to make sure no other wolf would touch her…ever. Both the Black Falls pack and Lily's pack from home all followed the same universal laws.

No enforcer entered another pack's territory without permission.

Which meant my alpha knew the Windbourn wolves were here. Which meant he knew Lily was here. And that was going to work to my advantage. My alpha was not an idiot. And having one of his enforcers mated to a Windbourn would make our pack stronger. I'd get no argument from him on what I planned to do.

Now I just needed to convince my sweet mate.

She trembled in my arms but didn't pull away. No. Her arms tightened around my waist. "I'm serious, Kade. I think something is wrong with me."

I pulled her down to sit beside me beneath a tree where the moss was thick and soft. A perfect bed on which to take her. "Tell me," I said, taking her hand, wanting the connection.

She glanced over her shoulder. "Shouldn't we keep moving? He'll follow me. He's probably following us right now. And he's not alone."

"No one will touch you, Lily," I vowed and I meant it. She searched my gaze for long seconds before settling next to me in an act that made me want to pound my chest with victory. Mine. She was mine. She trusted *me*. Wanted *me*. "He can follow all he wants, but he won't touch you."

But he would follow. This *Robert* who had her running

scared would not give up. Not that I could blame him or every unmated male in Black Falls. Unless I wanted to fight a half dozen challenges tonight, I had to take her to the Claiming. I had no choice. But first I would listen. "Tell me," I repeated.

"Robert. He's from East Springs. We dated. Went out. Whatever." She picked at the moss, looked up at me through her lashes. Even with the moon hidden by the thick forest, I could see her clearly. Her pale eyes, her round face, full lips. Even the hard points of her nipples through the thin white nightgown.

My teeth lengthened at the sight, but I pushed my wolf back. I would claim her, but not yet. I had to wait, follow the rules. Protect her with both my body and pack law. I had to wait, but not long. The moon would be at its apex soon. A few hours, and she'd be mine forever.

"He wanted me. He said he's been waiting for the time to be right."

A grunt escaped me at that bit of news. I knew exactly what he was waiting for, for Lily to be so out of her mind with lust and need that her wolf would force the woman to accept him. He must want her badly to take such a risk.

Because once the awakening was over and she came back to her senses? Well, no one could control a female werewolf full of rage. She probably would have killed him, and he would have deserved it. Add her blossoming power to the fact that she was a Windbourn and the wolf chasing her had to be out of his mind in love with her, or desperate.

"What did he do? Did he hurt you?" I'd kill him.

"No. But he wanted to come into my room. I don't even like him, but I…I pushed him away and fled."

I could scent her arousal, but it was tinged now with fear, with a lingering anger that was bitter on my tongue.

She shrugged. "That's the gist of it. I'm not really interested in going into detail. But he's here and based on the things he said, he's not going to leave."

I tensed. "What did he say?"

She licked her lips and I stifled a groan. "That he could smell me." She turned her head and lightly sniffed. No, she had no idea she was a wolf. I sighed quietly, realizing I had to tell her what she was and why Robert was after her. Why I wanted her. Why every fucking male in the area would want her.

And about the claiming ceremony that would make her mine forever.

"And…and he wanted to… to kiss me and touch me. He promised if I let him in he'd…"

Too well could I imagine what he'd said, and worse, what he'd been thinking. They were the same thoughts I was thinking now. Running my tongue over her flesh, tasting her nipples before going lower, to her sweet pussy and taking my fill. Hearing her cry out as I made her lose control over and over before burying myself balls deep and making her mine forever. I growled then and Lily startled. Lifting a hand to her face, I couldn't resist sliding my palm down her cheek to her neck, burying it in her hair. "I'm mad at him, not you. Never you. But you're mine now, Lily. I won't let him touch you."

She blinked slowly, leaning into my touch. I could see her struggle to find words, to battle the sensual needs fighting for command of her mind and body. Her wolf was close, ready to break free and run wild, unless Lily controlled her. If the wolf wasn't contained, Lily could go mad, or worse. She needed me, would need the dominant nature of my wolf to help her maintain control.

I ached to kiss her, but I didn't dare. If I started I would never stop. I settled for leaning closer and pressing my forehead to hers. She sighed, the sound soft. "Why is he here,

Kade? Why are you here? Why am I running through the forest in my nightgown? Why does my skin…hurt?"

I knew she wanted to ask more. The hunger to be touched would be strong now, making her body ache with need, her skin itself would crave contact. I couldn't take her, not yet. But I could help, if I was strong enough to resist temptation.

Leaning my back against the tree trunk I pulled her across my lap. The hand in her hair I left in place, wrapped around her neck, and used it to press her cheek to my chest right over my beating heart. Holding her felt natural, right. She settled instantly, curling into my heat as I ran my free hand up and down her spine in what I hoped would be a soothing gesture. I just had to hope she didn't feel my cock, thick and hard against her side.

I was a fucking saint. Here I was petting her when all I wanted was to throw her down on the ground and fuck her raw, fill her with my seed and tie her to me forever. The wolf in me wanted that so much so I had to count to a hundred before I could begin to explain.

"Your family, the Windbourns, has lived in Tennessee for a long time. Hundreds of years."

She nodded and I was relieved she knew at least this much of her family history. The werewolf migration had occurred even before the Declaration of Independence had been signed.

"They came from a long line of nobles in Europe, a family that was followed by horror stories, curses and legends."

"How do you know so much about us?" she asked.

"My family is from the same area. And we all suffered the same ancient curse."

CHAPTER 4

ade

LILY STIFFENED. "My family is not cursed."

"Have you not heard any strange legends? Rumors about your grandfather?"

Her silence was nearly deafening and I knew the answer. "What do you think he is, Lily?"

She shuddered. "Powerful. Strict. Everyone is afraid of him."

I couldn't help but chuff out a small laugh. I was amazed at how little she knew. "Are they? Are you sure about that? Aren't there those who come to him when they are in trouble and need help?"

"Yes. Almost everyone does that, but they're afraid of him, too. I can tell."

How the hell was I supposed to tell this beautiful woman that she was a werewolf? She wouldn't believe me. Then she'd panic and run, and things would go from bad to worse in a heartbeat.

"Why are they afraid of him?" I stroked over her silky hair. "Close your eyes and tell me the truth, no matter how crazy you think it sounds."

She shook her head and pulled away to look up at me. "No. Just tell me. All my life everyone around me has been keeping this big secret and it's driving me crazy. Just *tell me*. I'm tired of being the only one who doesn't know the truth. Is he in the mafia? A serial killer? An alien? What?"

"He's a werewolf, Lily. Perhaps the most powerful alpha in the world. And you're his granddaughter. Born or adopted?"

Her mouth dropped open and I saw her straight white teeth. "Born. My mom was his daughter." She said the words slowly and I was relieved that she wasn't dismissing my claim out of hand.

"He's a werewolf, from a long line of wolves. And you're his family, his blood, and part of his pack. You're a werewolf, too. They've just been waiting for your wolf to mature and come to the surface."

She was quiet for a minute, studying me, the tone of my words, the feel of my hands, even the beat of my heart.

"And that's what Robbie was waiting for? My wolf to wake up?" Her pale eyes met mine.

I nodded. "Yes. A female werewolf can't be claimed as a mate until her wolf accepts the pairing."

"That's insane." She denied me, but she didn't move. Her mind didn't grasp the extent of the truth yet, but deep down, she knew. Her wolf knew, therefore it remained quiet. "How would he know my inner werewolf was suddenly waking up? It's ridiculous."

"Can't you feel her moving inside you? The heat, the need

for touch, the lust that's so strong you can't think? That's not you, it's her."

I felt her shudder, and not from revulsion.

I ran my hand through her hair, but after that one shift of her body, it was like I was touching a statue. She was cold and unmoving as she worked through what I was saying. "Most female wolves awaken in their late teens. Some, like you, take longer. But there is no denying the call to mate, the scent of a female wolf in heat is nearly irresistible."

"In heat?" She scrambled from my lap and rose to her feet, glaring at me. She looked so beautiful in the moonlight, the nightgown revealing as much as it hid, her hair a dark curtain. Her eyes wide and wild. "In heat? Like I'm some kind of dog?"

I came to stand beside her, slowly so as not to startle her. "Robert was waiting for you to be ready, Lily. He's been waiting for this moment to make his claim when he knew you wouldn't be as likely to refuse him."

She glared at me, but there was hurt in her gaze. Hurt I wanted to kiss away. "Let's say I believe you about this werewolf business. I'm not stupid. I've seen things, heard rumors. I should be running screaming right now, but part of me knows it's true."

Relief coursed through my veins. She knew. Deep down and she was slowly accepting what she was. That meant she could accept me.

"I would never lie to you, Lily. I promise you that." I took a step closer but she backed away.

"What about you, Kade? How do I know you aren't exactly like Robbie? Is that what I am to you, too? A female in heat, ready to fuck? Am I just too horny to say no to you as well?" She curled in on herself, her arms wrapped around her waist as she took another step back.

"No." I let my wolf show, let the amber of my eyes darken to the color of my wolf. "I'm nothing like Robbie. I'm your mate. I will die to protect you, kill to possess you. You're mine and I'm yours. Even if you deny it, your wolf knows. She will fight to be with me. She'll be desperate and needy, Lily. Starving for touch, for her mate. For *me*. Why do you think you climbed out of your dorm and ran to me? Why do you ache for me at night? Oh, she'll accept another if you refuse me, but she wants me…just like you do." I held her gaze as I said the last because I wanted her to know I spoke the truth. "And I want you, Lily. I knew you were mine the moment I touched your hand on the side of the road."

She shook her head, her hair swirling about her pale shoulders. "This is crazy."

"I know." I held out my hand to her this time, gave her the choice. I would not force her, I could not. Her ice blue eyes were streaked with fire and the power of her wolf was upon her. I could hear the frantic beat of her heart, smell the tang of her need. I ached for a chance to taste it. Sate it. "Come with me, please. Let me touch you. Let me kiss you, Lily. I want you so badly, I can barely breathe. Be with me. Choose me. There is a claiming ceremony tonight. If I claim you there, Robbie will never come near you again. None of them will. Not even your grandfather will be able to reach you then."

"Why not?"

Moving slowly, I closed the distance between us and cupped her face with both hands because I needed to touch her. To hold her, even if just a little bit. "Because you'll be mine."

She looked into my eyes. "And is that what you want? To claim me?"

"Yes. I want you, Lily. So much it hurts." My entire body was strung tight as a bowstring until she nodded.

"Okay. I want you, too." She licked her lips. "What does

that mean? A claiming ceremony?"

"You'll be presented to the pack alpha. He'll ask you if you consent to the claiming ceremony. Once you agree, you'll be taken to a sacred place in the forest and I'll come for you."

"And then what?" She knew. I could see it in her eyes, but she needed me to say it.

"Then we'll be together." I leaned down and whispered the rest in her ear because I couldn't stare into her ice blue eyes and not lose my shit. "I'll kiss you everywhere, make you scream my name. And then I'll take you, fuck you until you can't take any more, until you beg for release, until you know exactly who you belong to."

"Yes." A shudder passed through her and into me, her nipples hardened into tight peaks pressed to my chest, her breathing short and fast and her arousal coating the wind like the sweetest perfume. My cock swelled to the point of bursting and I bit back a moan of pain. This woman, my woman, threatened my sanity, my years of iron will and self-discipline.

Nose buried against her neck now, my control nearly snapped. She was naked beneath her nightgown. I pulled back to resist the temptation to kiss her there, but that was a mistake. Her beautiful face was lit by moonlight, and she was looking at me with complete and absolute trust. I lowered my lips toward hers, unable to deny myself another moment.

A branch cracked behind me and I snapped to attention, Lily clinging to me once again. We were surrounded, and I cursed at myself for being so lost in my new mate that they'd sneaked up on us. It could have been worse. I knew the wolf hiding in the trees had made the sound as a courtesy. He was upwind, deadly quiet, and not alone.

"We have to go now, Lily."

She twisted out of my arms as five wolves emerged from the forest to surround us. She pressed her back to me and I put my hands on her shoulders. "It's all right. They're friends."

It was a small lie. Four I knew. One I did not, but by the hatred I saw in his eyes, this had to be Robbie, the werewolf who'd followed my Lily across a continent to claim her. But she was mine. The only way he'd ever lay a hand on her again was over my dead body.

<><><>

Lily, Two Hours Later

The cold night air caressed my overheated skin and caused tendrils of steam to float up from my flesh like tiny ghosts rising and dancing in the moonlight. I was naked beneath the robe, one they said was used for the traditional claiming. It was bright white and translucent, and fell to my feet in a silken wave. It was obviously meant to tease every male present with glimpses of my body. It left little to the imagination, but since it wasn't going to stay on for long, I wasn't going to think more about it.

God, this was insane.

Standing in the center of a small clearing, I tugged at the bonds about my wrists. No give. I could run, but there was nowhere to go. Nowhere to hide. And worse, I'd already agreed to this insanity. The Black Falls alpha, a man named Warren Sommerset, was an older man, close to sixty, with a barrel chest, massive arms and dark gray eyes that seemed to stare straight into my soul.

My Grandad had eyes like that, ice blue, but the same *don't try to bullshit me* stare. And when I'd met him earlier, with a glowering Robbie standing a few feet away and Kade next to me, I'd felt the urge to drop to my knees and bow my head to him, like he was a king.

Not a king, an alpha. And the wolf in me knew it.

I'd stayed on my feet, but I had a feeling it was only because I was still a Windbourn, and my pack loyalties remained back home with my family, the people I'd grown up with. I hadn't realized until that moment how deeply that connection ran within me. The strength of those bonds helped me stay on my feet, even when Kade and the others knelt beside me. Only Robbie and I remained on our feet, and the smug smile I saw on his face told me he knew the reason. I had a feeling he was counting on my loyalty to my grandfather, to our home, to influence my decision.

But Robbie was wrong. So wrong. I didn't care about the town, or my crusty old Grandad's non-existent empathy. I only wanted one wolf to touch me…and he wasn't here.

The meeting had ended over an hour ago. I'd been carted off by the women, bathed and fussed over until I was ready to scream.

And here I stood, surrounded by strangers, and I still couldn't make my body want the only familiar face among them. I realized now it was because neither me nor my wolf wanted him.

Male voices floated heavy on the night's breeze. I felt like a virgin sacrifice—ha! I was one—with only one other woman in sight to help me. She was already mated and not of interest to any of the males milling about, except perhaps her mate, who had to be nearby. I wasn't alone in this though. There were other female wolves being claimed tonight, although I'd only met one. Alana. She was standing next to the pack alpha, waiting her turn to be claimed and fucked by a werewolf. But she knew the rules, knew what was going on.

I was the lucky one who got to go first.

"Are you ready?" she asked. She walked over to me holding a long strip of black silk—another ceremonial thing—and it was going to cover my eyes. I wasn't sure if not being able to see would calm me or if not being able to see all the males circling and fighting for me—was I that much of a catch?—would make me panic. Alana's hands trembled worse than mine.

"No." I shook my head and searched the gathering crowd of single males. Where was Kade? He was the only one I was interested in, the only one I wanted touching me. Claiming me. *Fucking* me. Alana, who was from Black Falls and had grown up knowing this night would eventually come, told me many were here from neighboring packs to find a mate.

Now I knew why I could see so well at night. The wolf in me could see every male clearly as if it were noon, not close to midnight. They watched me, lust and need in their eyes as they inhaled deeply, picking up my scent, and the scents of other unmated females, on the air. They growled at one another like dogs fighting over a bone, and since I was up first, I was that bone. "I can't do this. This is crazy. Where's Kade?"

Alana wrapped her much cooler fingers around my bound hands and squeezed in a show of support. "Don't worry. A good man will claim you, a man who won't allow any of these weaklings to touch you."

I thought of Kade. His dark hair, full lips. Broad shoulders, intense gaze. God, everything about him made me hot, made me ache with need. Made my wolf almost prowl within. He'd held me, listened to me and I'd felt protected. Cherished. But when his gaze lowered to my lips, when he told me what he wanted to do to me, I felt desired. Craved.

Was he out there? I didn't see him, didn't sense him like I had when I looked out my dorm window. I'd felt…relief and happiness rolled into one at the sight of him. As if I were coming home. He'd said I was his mate and my wolf preened at the idea. I'd barely even talked to him, but I knew. He *was* my mate, yet I didn't see him. Would he leave me here, allow me to be claimed by someone else? He wouldn't. He *couldn't* if we really was my mate.

Alana patted my hand, bringing me out of my thoughts. Worrisome thoughts. I appreciated my new friend's efforts to reassure me, but I wasn't convinced. What if something happened? My inner wolf—that's what Kade said drove me now that I was in heat—wanted him, but what if it was wrong? What if it turned out Kade was just like Robert? What if I didn't really want him at all? What if I was just in heat, exactly like a stupid poodle?

CHAPTER 5

 ily

MY WOLF NUDGED MY THOUGHTS, telling me I was wrong, that it wanted Kade. That he was the one for me. For us. God! I had a wolf in me. I shook my head in continued disbelief, but here I was, mostly naked in the middle of a serious wolf claiming ceremony.

"Explain to me again why this is happening to me," I said to Alana. She understood. She'd known her whole life she was a shifter. She offered me a small smile.

"I don't know your specifics, but wolf science says tonight is the first full moon since you've reached the Age of Ascension."

I must have given her a funny look because she laughed.

"Have you been all hot and bothered the last few days?"

I nodded, blushing at how I'd made myself come in my sleep. Once, but it hadn't been like this.

"The Age of Ascension is wolf-speak for the time the

wolfy bits inside you come to life," she continued. "You'll be able to shift soon, but you'll need a mate to help you control your wolf. The presence of a strong alpha is enough. But for women, it's different. We will only submit to one male, and that's generally our mate. You're going to shift soon, Lily. You're of the age to be claimed, to belong to someone, just as they will belong to you. Tonight, you'll be mated to one of the single males, and that male has until sunrise to convince you to keep him. You can resist, a few have. Just last month in fact, when the alpha's daughter rejected the male who'd tried to claim her. It was the first time in two decades a male's claim has been denied."

My eyebrows went up in surprise. I had no idea if it was good or bad, but at least I could say no, right?

"The male who claims you will have to woo you with his strength, his skill, and his touch. No words are allowed. Here, drink this."

Alana held up a small cup, which I took from her with my bound hands.

"What is it?" I asked, sniffing it. It smelled like tea.

"An herbal concoction that the healers make."

I put it to my lips, took a sip, then another. It was sweet, like sugared tea.

"It will guarantee that no child will result from the evening's activities."

Oh. My. God. Through all this insanity, I never considered a baby. I wasn't on the pill or any other kind of birth control. I took a big swig, ensuring the liquid would work. Good. While I wanted kids, I didn't want to make one tonight. With a stranger. No, even with Kade, I didn't want to make a baby tonight. I needed to know him first. Not just my wolf, but me.

"You'll spend the next few hours blindfolded and seduced by one of the hot hunks milling around."

No big deal at all, right? Blindfolded, bound, mostly naked and then fucked. Yeah. No big deal.

I should have been terrified, but all I could do was wish Kade would hurry.

"Trust me, they can scent your heat, your arousal and they want you." She glanced around the clearing, her calm assessment of the men present strangely reassuring. She knew these men, had grown up with them. "Kade will come for you, Lily. And he'll treat you right. If any of these guys didn't, they'd get taken down by the Accalia."

"The Accalia?"

Alana smiled and there was mischief in her eyes. "Yes. Every pack has an alpha male that's in charge. He is responsible for the pack's protection and for keeping the males in line. But the Accalia is the matriarch. She's part pack mother, part Supreme Court judge. Her word is law in all internal pack business, family business. She gives a banishment or execution order, and no one blinks."

Holy shit. Who was my Grandad's Accalia?

My mother. I knew it with a certainty that made me proud and suddenly years of odd looks and awkward glances at the grocery store made a whole lot more sense. And since my mother's death? I had no idea. "Shouldn't the matriarch be the alpha's mate?"

Alana laughed at that. "Not necessarily. Sometimes the alpha's mate is too nice. I mean, seriously. Can you imagine yourself giving a kill order? Or banishing someone you've known all your life?"

No, I couldn't. I tended to mend fences and put up with more bullshit than was strictly good for me. Hence a dating history with Robbie that had gone on a lot longer than it should have. "Who's your Accalia?"

Alana smiled. "My sister, Sonia. She's only a few years older than me, but she's mean as hell and doesn't take any bullshit. I want to be like her when I grow up." She winked at me and I smiled back. "Don't worry. She'll interview you tomorrow, when this is all done, just to make sure you're okay and to welcome you into the pack. Choose Kade or someone else. It's up to you. Whoever you choose will treat you right. Trust me, these guys want you. You smell like their favorite treat right now."

I blushed at that. For wolves, scenting each other was hot. For me, not so much. At least it never had been, but I could still almost taste the scent of Kade's skin on my tongue. I wanted to taste him for real.

"But how do I know if I really want them? Him. The One." I licked my lips. "I mean, my ex is stalking me and I was drawn to him. My mate-meter is a little out of whack."

"Don't worry," she soothed. "You'll know. Your wolf knows."

I wasn't so sure about that, but there wasn't anything to be done.

"Yeah, but tied up?" I held my bound wrists up. "Blindfolded? This seems a little much, don't you think?"

"A wolf mating is intense. You will submit, mind, body and soul to your new mate. Knowing your wrists are bound, that you can't see, will remind your wolf of this submission. And she won't surrender to just anyone. Trust me. She's going to go wild. You're going to need those."

Submit to my new mate? Old fashioned, much?

The male murmurs stopped and the clearing became quiet. Alana lifted her chin, took on a serious bearing as she stepped behind me and placed a cool hand on my shoulder. "Kneel, Lily Windbourn, and choose a mate."

Choose a mate?

I couldn't help but laugh at that. Was that a joke? But any humor died on my lips when her hand prompted me to drop to my knees in the soft earth. I took a deep breath, glanced around one more time, looking for a suspiciously absent Kade in the clearing, before the black silk covered my eyes, blinding me to vanity. And everything else.

Alana whispered one last reassurance my ear, "He'll come for you. Don't worry."

God, I hoped so. This wasn't how I expected to lose my virginity, but if it had to be this way, in a forest clearing, I wanted it to be with Kade. But where was he?

I will die to protect you, kill to possess you. You're mine and I'm yours.

His words gave me comfort, but what if he'd changed his mind?

I shuddered and tested the strength of the bonds around my hands. Not unbreakable, not for a werewolf like myself, but the submission they symbolized suddenly chafed. I didn't want any male but Kade touching me and I knew Robert was out there. I'd seen him milling about when I met with the alpha. He'd been like a shadow. Everywhere the women took me for preparation, he followed like a puppy.

But he was no cute, cuddly Labrador pup. He was big and hard and strong, and my wolf's hackles raised at the thought of him touching me. I didn't want him. I wanted Kade.

Alana said I had the power to reject any man who wanted to claim me. If someone besides Kade touched me, I could survive the night's seduction by rejecting whichever male was unlucky enough to try.

If they thought I was going to just roll over and spread my legs, they hadn't met Lily Windbourn.

"Who would claim Lily Windbourn this night? Challengers, step forward." The command boomed through the small clearing and silence descended over the woods. Not even crickets chirped as the pack alpha, Warren, raised his voice to carry over the slight breeze.

Alana gave my shoulder one last squeeze and walked away,

leaving me to face my fate and the males eager to tame me. There was movement and my heart pounded as I heard the preliminary sounds of fighting. The sound of fists striking flesh, bone. Grunts of pain, ragged breathing. I was glad I was on my knees, for I was suddenly scared. I couldn't see, couldn't defend myself. I cowered, trying to make myself as small as possible. My ears worked just fine as a group of males jostled, growled, and threatened each other. They were all fighting over me?

I wanted to roll my eyes, but the effect would've been completely lost behind the black silk. All I had to do was survive the night and choose Kade as my mate. Would I be allowed to tie him down and claim *him?* Would Kade allow me to be in control? I knew the Windbourn males were alpha through and through and I sensed it in him as well. But to dominate over a mate? I was eager to find out. If I could get through this ceremony.

The shuffling, growling and posturing noises died down and I held my breath. My heart pounded, my palms were damp.

"Three warriors would make a claim this night. So be it." The alpha's powerful voice quieted the forest again. "Let their names be written in the archive."

Archive? It was almost medieval, this process. So formal. Why didn't someone just toss me over his shoulder and carry me away? But these weren't cavemen, they were shifters and it seemed they followed a whole bunch of strange customs to ensure everyone knew who a mate belonged to. Kade promised that if he claimed me tonight, there would be no doubt as to my mate. That even my Grandad would not be able to reach me.

There would be no challenge to a mating. Mates were sacred. Protected by all pack laws. His alpha, Warren, had confirmed it. I just had to trust Kade to come for me.

I heard the dutiful scratching of a pen, and then a pregnant silence that stressed my nerves to nearly breaking before the alpha spoke again. Three males were willing to fight each other for the right to touch me. Three! Goose bumps broke out over my flesh and I shivered in the cold night air. Anticipation, or dread? I wasn't sure which.

One could be Kade, but how would I know him from the other two? How did I resist them when my skin ached to be touched, when my core throbbed with need and my entire body would melt in surrender at his first touch? My wolf was awake and prowling, hungry. So hungry, as if she'd been starved for decades and had a feast before her. She wanted to consume and be consumed.

"Wolves, you know the rules. Break them, and you will be executed. Foreign brothers, we will give no quarter to you should you step out of bounds."

My chest squeezed. Foreign brothers? Males from another pack were here, surely he was talking to Robbie. Others, too? Males who were about to touch me...unless. I straightened my shoulders and pictured Kade's broad chest, perfect jaw and piercing amber eyes. It was his hooded gaze I imagined boring into my soul as the alpha finally addressed me directly.

"Lily Windbourn of the East Springs pack, we honor you this night. Three fine wolves would claim you as mate. They have the right to know if your heart still beats in your chest, or if it travels with another." Truth in all things. That was the pack way. The men had the right to know if the woman they attempted to claim was in love with another man. Didn't mean it would stop them, but they would know what they were up against.

I thought of Kade. I didn't love him, did I? I hardly knew him. But I ached for him, wanted him to be my mate, to claim me. Did I need him? Crave him? Demand him? Absolutely.

Was that what love was? Did the need to belong to Kade mean I'd given him my heart? I hadn't even known it had happened, but yes. My heart belonged to him.

I licked my lips. "No heart beats in my chest, alpha. It has been given away."

A murmuring wove over those in attendance. "And is the wolf you would prefer as mate here this night?"

I hung my head, ashamed and embarrassed by the truth. I couldn't see him. I couldn't scent him. I couldn't even *feel* Kade nearby. "I don't know."

A low growl sounded from one of the three who stood just a few feet before me. Great. Somebody loved a challenge. Even those who weren't actually pack alpha behaved like alpha males.

Warren proceeded with the ceremony and addressed the warriors present. "Knowing her heart belongs to another, do you still wish to claim her?"

Could it be that easy? Would they walk away? Leave me to rip off the blindfold, tug off the bindings and go find Kade?

The alpha's sigh dashed that small hope. "So be it. Even with your heart given to another, two warriors remain and they claim the Right of Initiation."

Surely Kade was one of them. He promised he'd be with me, that he would be the one to claim me. He *had* to be one of them.

"What is the Right of Initiation?" I asked.

More whispers filled the open space. I wasn't sure if it was because I spoke or because I didn't know what it was.

"The two males offer initiation to their touch with single a kiss," the alpha replied.

I raised my head, hope filling me, making me dizzy. One

kiss. If I didn't respond to something so trivial, they'd walk away. No suffering through hours of lust and agony, denying the male any true pleasure. One kiss each. I could do that. I had to know Kade from a kiss, right?

But no. He'd never kissed me. And why was that? We'd been alone, touching. He said he wanted me. But why hadn't he kissed me? I had no idea what he would feel like, taste like...

"Proceed," the alpha instructed.

CHAPTER 6

ily

THE FIRST MALE approached and knelt before me. I couldn't see him, but I felt his presence, heard his breathing. I waited, lips tilted up expectantly. He didn't make me wait long before his hot hands grabbed my shoulders and pulled me forward into the kiss. I gasped as his lips met mine. They were firm, hot, and skilled, but they did not make me feel anything, and I did not open my mouth to him. The smell of his skin was familiar, as was the feel of his hands.

Robbie.

The knowledge chilled me and I became stiff as iron in his hold.

Ha! Success. I was not drawn to him, felt no desire, therefore he would not claim me. But where was Kade? He'd promised no other would touch me.

"Enough!" The alpha's voice rang through the clearing and the lips left mine in defeat.

Yes, defeat, for I'd been thinking throughout the kiss. I wanted blind passion, a male that would strip my thoughts as well as my body.

A growl escaped the male above me, dark. Angry. But a different growl, deeper, menacing, followed directly after. I didn't fear for my safety—there were enough witnesses to keep me safe—I only feared that the sun would rise and I'd be mated to the wrong wolf.

Where was Kade? When Alana put the blindfold on me, he'd been absent from the group of men around me. He'd told me he had to go talk to the alpha before the claiming ceremony, but the alpha was here. Where was Kade?

I wanted to say I was sorry for feeling nothing as I listened to Robbie coming to his feet, but I wasn't. I didn't want him kissing me. Especially when I was bound and at his mercy. I would submit, I ached to do so, but not to him. I felt disappointment roll off him in waves, but I didn't care. He wasn't the one. He wasn't *mine*.

With a taut anger about him, he stepped away when the other male present growled another warning, one who acted like he was already my mate, like he had rights.

The sound, the vibrations of his growl reverberated through me. Sent goosebumps down my arms.

Bodies moved, shifted and I felt the second male's presence before me. I braced myself for the second kiss, the key to my freedom. If his mouth was upon mine, I would know immediately it was not to be. But it didn't come. One minute stretched into an agony of two, and then three as he knelt before me but did nothing. I would swear I could actually feel his gaze traveling over my skin. And he'd be able to see it all through the teasing robe. My hard nipples, the trimmed dark hair at the apex of my thighs. The garment left nothing to the imagination. Allowed them to be tempted, yet blatantly aware of a female's offerings. It seemed they always knew exactly what they were trying to claim.

I could hide nothing, not even my heart.

Tension built in the air between us like an electrical storm of lust that bit into my sensitive skin. The male's mating heat soaked into my muscles, tempted me to be soft, to melt into his touch. This male wanted me badly. I'd never felt this heat, but the claimed women I'd met before the ceremony spoke of it fondly. The tingling warmth and the sex. Steaming hot, incredible, blow-your-mind sex.

My nipples refused to listen to my mind and hardened to tight peaks as his heat wrapped around me and invaded all the way to my core.

"Are you going to kiss me?" I asked.

He said nothing.

"Well?" I whimpered, needing to know. What was this I was feeling? Where was it coming from? The male before me or from somewhere—or someone—else?

"Silence!" the Alpha boomed, startling me. I wobbled on my knees and a hand settled on my shoulder, letting me regain my balance. The heat from it searing.

I shrugged off his touch, afraid of it. If it wasn't Kade, I didn't want it. I didn't want to feel anything toward him. Especially the spark that came from his quick assistance.

No. I didn't want this man. "I want you to kiss me," I whispered, my voice tempered so low I had to hope only the male before me could hear. I didn't really *want* the kiss, but I wanted to know. I had to know and the answer was in the kiss.

I ached. Whimpered, disappointment cutting through me. Why wouldn't he kiss me?

Warm, firm hands slid along my jaw on both sides of my face and I gasped, surprised by the touch, surprised by the heat of it. Cradling my head as gently as if he held fine china, he held me still for...finally, his kiss.

Where the first man had been firm and skilled, this kiss was a slow tasting that started at the corner of my mouth. Instead of pulling me forward as the first male had done, he held me in place, kept me away from the lure of his heated body. Somehow, knowing it was there, just out of reach made me ache to rub against him, to lift my bound hands and touch, to cling. To never let go.

I whimpered.

The male didn't care if it was because I was pleased or repulsed. He tilted my head to the side and ran his tongue over my lips, tasting me. Continuing with his onslaught. With a moan, I opened my mouth to him, unable to fight the urge to taste his strength, his desire for me, just a little bit.

Yes, it was the heat taking over, confusing me. I wanted his touch, his lips on me. His heated hands. I wanted more. But was he Kade? How could I not know?

With a growl, he pulled me forward and invaded my mouth with his tongue. All pretense of seduction was gone, the kiss turned into an aggressive assault that demanded submission. And I wanted to give it. I softened then, like wax in the sun.

My body responded by becoming a living flame and I arched against him, burning up inside. And it was just a kiss! My pussy lips throbbed with need to the point of pain and the cold night air wafted over my now wet core with a chilling breeze, alerting me to my utter failure.

I wasn't cold. I wasn't indifferent to this male. One kiss and this stranger had defeated me, owned me, made me long for his touch in a way Kade never had. But then, Kade had never had the chance. There hadn't been enough time for him to do so.

"Enough." The Alpha's command straightened my spine

and I pulled away from the kiss, disgusted with my lack of control. I turned my head away from him as the Alpha continued, "The Right of Initiation has decided the matter. Write this male's name in the Archive, and let us move on to the next claiming."

I felt more than heard the remaining males leave this first area of the ceremonial grounds. It was done. This male, whoever he was, had been given the right to try to claim me. I could refuse him, as Alana had said another had done, but how could I resist? If I almost came from a kiss, what would I do, how would I submit when he put his hands on my body? I ached for him to do so. Needed it. I didn't *want* to resist.

For the next few hours I'd be alone, naked under the stars with this male as he used every skill and trick he had to seduce me into accepting him. I didn't think he'd need to resort to trickery. I was like putty in his hands. Hot, eager putty. The chill night air would offer no help, as we were both more than human and the cold would have no effect on either of us. Instead, the night would actually assist the male's cause, calling to my wild nature. At least that was what Alana had told me. I would want to be claimed out in the open air, beneath the full moon. It seemed a little flaky at the time, but now, it was all too true.

Human men hadn't satisfied my physical needs and because of it, there had been no risk to my heart or soul. Now I knew why I'd never been interested in anyone from high school, or any of the guys from home. *He* wasn't there. He wasn't the one for me. Unless…

No. This male couldn't be Robbie. I'd denied him for so long, I couldn't all of a sudden crave him. The heat was strong, but not like this. No. I had no idea who this male was, but it wasn't him.

But was it Kade? How could I feel *everything* for Kade only a few hours ago and even more for this male? Whoever he was would take nothing less than total surrender, and if I gave that to him, my heart would go with it.

He still held me, palm wrapped around my neck in a display of total dominance. He could break my neck with a flick of his wrist, but his thumb traced my jawline with a feather soft touch instead. I could somehow feel his eyes inspecting his prize, assessing me in a new light now that he had the right to touch me, to make me come. To do whatever he wished with me.

When the last spectator had gone onto the next claiming and the clearing absolutely silent except for the whisper of the wind through the leaves overhead, I turned my face back to him with an apology.

"I'm sorry. I can't be yours."

He leaned in until his lips brushed my ear and whispered so softly I barely heard him. No, my wolf heard him. "We'll see."

I gasped. A male wasn't allowed to speak. That's what I'd been told, that speaking was a clear violation of the rules, but this male didn't seem to care. His hands roamed from my neck to my shoulders, over my collarbones and lower to slide over the tops of my breasts through the robe. Much to my delight and disappointment, they didn't linger but continued down to my bound hands. It was as if he was feeling what he'd had his eyes on. A tactile inspection and I had to wonder if he found me worthy.

He wrapped his hands around mine—they seemed so big—and pulled me carefully to my feet, then lifted me into his arms and carried me like a groom carrying a bride over the threshold. Such a quaint human custom, but still, I felt my cheeks flush as he settled me on the feather filled mat used for the true claiming and laid me down. No sooner were my shoulders on the soft surface than he pulled my bound hands over my head and secured them to the post placed there for that very purpose. Now my chest thrust up at him like a wanton offering, the robe parting and I knew he could see the inside curves of my breasts and even my pussy. My hands were restrained above my head and I was completely at his mercy. I couldn't cover myself, couldn't do anything but submit. The thought wasn't nearly as upsetting as it should've been. The more time that passed, the more I wanted to give myself to him.

He laid down beside me, running his fingers up and down the gap in the front of my gown. Rough fingertips grazed my skin, lingered and explored the softness of my flesh from my neck to the valley of my breasts, over the soft planes of my stomach to the top of my pussy, then back up. Nothing more, just up and down, back and forth. Playing. Learning. Watching. I lay panting and helpless as he built a slow fire I was afraid I wouldn't be able to extinguish. Sweat bloomed on my skin.

Then he whispered again. "Who is this male you pine for?" He lowered his head and placed a soft, chaste kiss on my hard nipple. I gasped. I couldn't help it, for I'd never had someone do that before. It felt so good and I arched my back toward him, wanting more.

"And why is he not here to claim your perfection for his own?"

Shaking my head, I remained silent. There was no good answer to that question. I would not bare my soul to this male and confess my faults. I turned my head to the side, away from him, despite the fact that it bared the side of my neck like a sacred offering, an offering he didn't hesitate to accept. With a low rumble, he nuzzled my neck with his nose and lips, nibbled his way to my collarbone and teased me with little nips of his teeth. His heat covered me as he threw one leg over my thigh, his knee between my legs to hold me in place, to tug me wider and more open for his touch. Not that I could go anywhere. I tugged at the bindings about my wrist to confirm this.

Alana said the alpha's daughter had resisted her suitor for an entire night? Good God, the woman had to have a will of iron.

The hard length of his cock pressed into my hip through his pants. He was so big and I had to wonder if he'd fit. Would it hurt? Surely, something of that size would rip me in two. But my train of thought veered away from worry when his hand massaged my breast with a firm touch. His thumb brushed over my wet nipple and the action left me breathless. My body ached for this man's touch, my wet pussy clenched, needed to be filled and my entire body arched beneath him in invitation.

"Please," I whispered. I bit my lip. I shouldn't have responded. I knew it in my head, but my heart and my body refused to listen to my mind. The wolf was in control now, and the thinking part of me was rapidly losing ground. The fierce desire to submit filled me and I knew it was a lost cause as his mouth trailed kisses over my jaw and hovered at the corner of my mouth.

"Tell me," he said, but I didn't know what. "Who owns your heart?"

Everywhere his body touched mine, heat flared between us and soaked into my muscles. Fire filled my veins and I longed to rub against him, to explore every inch of huge, hard, muscular male. I fought the bonds, fought his body's pressing hold. I was becoming wild with need. He knew just how to build it, a little at a time so as not to scare me. No one had ever made her feel like this. No one. Well, no one but Kade.

This was just sex. Pure lust. I had to resist or I could be stuck with a male who lit my body on fire but left my heart cold.

He kissed me then, a long leisurely exploration of my mouth with his tongue. He had all night to taste and explore, to seduce me. And he was doing a pretty good job of it. He was really, really difficult to resist. Everything he did, everywhere he touched, how soft, hard, gentle, persuasive, I liked. No, I loved. I moaned in response, my body on fire for his touch. I had to stop.

"Tell me," he repeated.

"Kade. I want Kade." I managed to whisper against his lips, between kisses that were stealing my soul piece by piece, weakening every bit of my resistance. Was that what he'd wanted from me? "I will only give my virginity to him."

The male stopped his sensual assault and I felt his warm breath fan my neck as he growled. I shivered from the possessive sound. He whispered once more against my ear.

"You are untouched?"

I nodded my head.

"Do you love him?"

Heart racing in my chest like a frightened bird's, I debated. Should I tell this male the truth? If I succumbed, and he claimed me, would he seek Kade out in challenge? He would have the right to do so and to kill Kade if he so much as spoke to me after the claiming. But what if he let me go? What if he released me from the ritual?

He must have sensed my thoughts. "I give you my word I will not challenge him if you tell me the truth." His hand slid down over my stomach in a slow sensual glide. "I want to know who you want...here, filling you for the first time and making you come."

As he spoke, he slid two long fingers into my tight pussy and I gasped at the extreme pleasure as he slowly moved them in and out in a hot, very wet glide. I was tight and I felt a twinge of pain, but I loved it. I ached for his touch, but his fingers wouldn't do. No, I wanted more. I wanted his hot body to cover mine, to wrap my legs around his hips and surge against him as he buried his cock inside me, making me truly his. Not as a wolf claiming his mate, but as a man took a woman. Stretched her open, felt her tight heat adjust to his cock, to know he was the only one to have ever been there. To know she belonged solely to him. Either way, man or wolf, I wanted to be fucked without mercy until I screamed my release.

I wasn't a shy virgin. I just hadn't given myself to anyone because it had never been like this. When a cock filled me for the first time, I wasn't going to be passive. No, I was going to come. Hard.

Game over. Trembling with need, I acknowledged the truth and my very obvious weakness. I wouldn't be able to resist this man. This wolf. He was heat and fire to my cold heart, and if he didn't stop voluntarily, I would succumb. I couldn't lie to myself. The truth was the only thing that might stop him from claiming me. Perhaps he was a worthy male, a man and wolf I could grow to love as well as lust after, but only if I knew for certain Kade didn't want me.

"Kade. Yes. My heart is his. I know it's crazy, but yes, I love him. Please let me go."

The male froze into a solid block of ice above me, stopped breathing for several seconds, then growled a protest into my ear. "Did he tell you he wanted to claim you?"

"Yes."

"Has he touched you, or kissed you, or done this?" His mouth latched onto my nipple through the sheer fabric of my robe as he resumed fucking me with his fingers in a firm, take-no-prisoners assault on my clit and core.

CHAPTER 7

*L*ily

"No. There was no time. We've barely had time together, but I *know*. I can't deny how I respond to you, but I want him." My hips bucked beneath his skilled touch, needing more. Harder. Faster. Bigger. Heaven help me, I wanted his cock stretching me, pounding into me as he fucked me senseless. A single tear slipped from the corner of my eye and was instantly absorbed into the black silk still covering my eyes. "Please, if you don't stop I will betray the man I love."

"I smell your tears, Lily." His touch gentled as he slid from me, his fingers sliding over the wet folds of my pussy as if learning my contours. With a raspy voice, as if he were teetering on the very edge of losing control, his murmured, "You truly love him? Even though, as you say, you've barely had time together?"

I nodded my head, licked my lips. "Yes. I do." I turned my head away from his kiss and spoke the truth. "If you claim me tonight, if you take what doesn't belong to you, I can never truly be yours. I'm so sorry. I was stupid. I didn't tell him how I felt when I had the chance and now I have caused both of us pain. I don't know why I can't seem to resist your touch, but my heart can never be yours."

He kissed me softly, reverently on the stomach and spoke to me with a man's voice, a voice he no longer tried to hide with barely whispered words and the cadence of a stranger. "I told you no one else would touch you, Lily. You're mind and I'm yours. Forever."

Shock rippled through me in waves and I stilled, like a rabbit caught in a predator's sight, assessing the danger. Kade? Was I hearing things? Were my senses so clouded with lust that my own body would trick me? Lust cooled to ice as I considered the possibility, then roared back with twice the heat. I tugged at the bonds above me, gathering my will to shred them, to break free and rip the silk from my eyes. I needed to see…

"Kade?"

"Hush." His hand slid up the bare length of my arm in a tender caress and stilled my hands, relaxed the storm gathering in my muscles. "Yes, it's me."

Heart racing triple speed, I still didn't trust my traitorous body. I was too hot, too out of control, to believe my senses. "Prove it."

He nibbled at my lips as he answered. "You came to me from your dorm room, like an angel, your white nightgown billowing around you. You were mine then and you are mine now. I knew it the first time I touched you wearing that pink sundress on the side of the road."

It was him, and this time, when I said his name, it was filled with relief, happiness and desperation. It was him, he was here with me, over me.

With one swift thrust, his fingers were back inside me as

his palm rubbed my clit and his tongue plunged in and out of my mouth in a matching rhythm. His name left my lips again, this time as a moan and I came apart in his arms, pushed to climax now that I knew who held me, who touched me and demanded surrender.

My soft cry was captured by his lips as he pumped his fingers in and out of my wet pussy, pushing me over the edge once again. Shaking all over, I whimpered in protest when his fingers left me empty and pulsing with the need to be filled completely. I needed more. I needed to be claimed.

His kiss traveled lower, to my breasts. He suckled one nipple then the other, tormenting me with pleasure until I bucked and writhed beneath him.

"Kade, please."

Hot and wet, his tongue slid down to tease the sensitive skin around my navel, then the jutting curve of my hip. He pulled the soft gown to my sides, baring me completely from the neck down. "Do you want me, Lily?"

"How can you ask that? I've been begging."

"But you are a virgin. You wish to not only be claimed by me, but give me that precious gift?"

His words slid over me reverently, just like the tips of his fingers, the soft feel of his lips.

"Yes!" I twisted, once again testing the bonds, sensing I could break it if I gathered my strength. I wanted my hands in his hair. I needed to feel the strength of his shoulders and the angles of his back when he filled me, when he stretched me wide, pounded into my eager flesh for the first time and claimed me forever. "I want to touch you."

"Not yet." His hands pushed my knees wide and I knew he knelt between them with a clear view of my pussy. The cold night air blew across the sensitive area, emphasizing just how open and exposed I was to him. He could see all of me. Hear me, feel me.

"You are so fucking beautiful." The hand resting on the inside of my right knee glided smoothly up my inner thigh to explore me gently. I didn't want gentle. I *needed* more, I needed to be fucked, to know I belonged to him, to *feel* him dominate me, to fill me with his cock and make me his.

"Please."

"Say my name." He slowly stretched me, three fingers this time, as if to prepare me for his cock, while the thumb of his opposite hand pressed against my throbbing clit.

"Kade." I shifted beneath his touch, straining to take more of him, to feel more.

"Say it again." He pulsed in and out of me, stronger this time, his fingertips bumping the very tip of my womb. And he was hot, so hot. The heat his body generated extended several feet like a bonfire. It melted my resistance, bathed me in his lust.

"Kade. Please." The growl in my voice surprised me, but I didn't have to hold myself in check, didn't need to worry about taming the wild side of my desire with him. Instead, I released the passion from the deep, dark place I'd always been afraid to touch. I stopped fighting and let him see into my very soul as I begged him over and over to take me, to fuck me, to make me come.

With a growl, he lowered his head to my pussy and laved there, devoured and tasted me with his tongue and mouth until I shattered again, sobbing his name, spinning higher and higher until I was no longer in control. I was mindless hunger and pure animal lust. Nothing would satisfy me but his cock buried to the balls, pounding into my pussy as hard and fast as he could go, filling me with his seed and claiming me as his once and for all.

With a scream, I tore my hands free of the binding above my head, ripped off my blindfold and buried them in his hair, locking him to my pussy as his tongue stabbed deep and his growl vibrated against my clit like a vibrator set on high.

Another orgasm crashed through me, driving me to madness. I needed him inside me. *Now.*

I knew my eyes had gone animal as inhuman strength flooded my limbs and I lunged forward, stretching him out and tackling him beneath me on the mat. My victory was short lived, as he immediately wrapped me in his arms and rolled on top of me once again. His hard cock pressed against the entrance to my pussy and I bucked beneath him, desperate.

In response, he slid his length up and down my wet entrance, teasing us both.

"Say my name." One more demand, but his voice was hoarse with need, with the effort it cost him to stay in control. I didn't want him in control, I wanted him wild.

"Kade."

"I'm claiming you, Lily. Your virginity, your heart. Your soul."

"Yes," I breathed, arching my hips for him.

With one smooth thrust he entered me, stretched me, filled me so full I was afraid I'd explode with pleasure. My inner walls rippled around him, adjusting. He was so big, so much longer and thicker than his fingers. Hot, yet hard like a steel beam. I gasped at the intrusion, shifted my hips to take him deeper, until his body trembled above my own.

He held himself still only briefly, kissing my temple and ensuring I was all right. But all at once his wolf took over. He held nothing back as he filled me and withdrew, a human piston moving in and out of my wet heat. The sound of our fucking filled the air, mixed with my cries of pleasure, his growl of possession. I opened my legs wider and ground my hips against his body, meeting every thrust with a demand of my own. Our fingers entwined and he trapped my hands in his grasp on either side of my head, lowered his mouth to kiss me as his body plunged into mine over and over.

His heat intensified like an inferno blazed around us, until I could barely breathe. An answering psychic heat rose from deep within my heart to claim him. The Bond. We weren't human. This wasn't just fucking. This was mating, a claiming. This was unbreakable. Forever.

"Mine." His eyes glowed as he pushed harder, deeper into sensitive flesh and I moaned beneath him. He grinned and I saw the sharp glint of his teeth in the moonlight. The canines were longer than normal. But I didn't think about what that meant for the pleasure was too great. But when he lowered his head and I felt the white stab of pain at the juncture of my shoulder and neck, I knew the truth.

This was the claiming. I screamed with the pain of it, squirmed to escape, but it was instantly gone, for a bright heat flared through my body, centered on my pussy and I came again. It was like nothing I'd ever felt before. A merging, as if I was sensing Kade's pleasure as well, as if the connection between us was finally opened. We were one.

There was no fighting the tidal wave of sensation as the bond locked into place and we came apart in each other's arms. His cock pulsed deep within me, filling and marking me with his seed.

The claim was made. The bite, the seed deep inside me proved it. All other males could scent Kade's claim, could see the mark on my shoulder. I was his. And yes! He was mine. His cock was hard inside me, but he released his bite on my flesh, then licked the wound. I felt no pain there. While I knew the wound remained it seemed to be quickly healing. Finally, he lifted his head, looked down at me as he caught his breath. Blood was on his lips. My blood. And lower, between my legs, I knew his seed would be tinged with my virgin blood as well.

WILD WOLF CLAIMING

I was his.

And yet, I reveled in the knowledge that he was mine forever. No other would ever turn his head, or touch him, or kiss his perfect mouth, or have his huge cock pumping into her with wild abandon.

With a sigh, I waited for my heart to slow, for my body to stop tingling. "I love you, Kade." I knew it was crazy. I'd only known him a few days, but he'd been there for me, taken care of me, made me feel safe and beautiful and worshipped. The only thing I saw when I looked into his eyes was raw desire, possession, need. It wasn't love, but it was a start.

Still buried within me, he nuzzled my neck with soft lingering kisses and worked his way to my lips, which were still swollen and sensitive from his possession. His thumb brushed over my cheek. "I love you, Lily. You're mine now. Forever. And I'm going to make sure you know it."

"But..." Sixty seconds ago, I would've sworn I was too tired to move, but as he shifted his cock inside me, thick and ready to go again, desire roared back to life and I moved against him, teasing him, tempting him, hoping he would make me scream his name once more.

My eyes must have gone wolf, because he chuckled before he withdrew.

"What?" I reached for him, but he shook his head and flipped me over onto my stomach. I felt his seed trickle from me, knew I was well and truly claimed. My pussy was sore, but I loved the feel, knowing it meant he was mine. That my pussy was definitely *his*.

"Now, my love, now your wolf will know as well."

As if I—she—had any doubt.

My pussy clenched in response to his words and he wasted no time, simply lifted my hips into the air and entered me from behind. My wolf howled with pleasure and a strange sound escaped my own throat at the sweet invasion, his path eased by his seed. I lay my head on the mat and closed my eyes, content to let him love me, for once the wild fire inside me tamed to a submissive heat. He was dominant, and wolf, and mine. I took a deep breath, gave over to him. Yielded. My wolf practically howled with happiness.

He loved me with slow, leisurely strokes, shifting my hips until he hit the sensitive spot inside I had no idea was there and I mewled like a cat, so hot I couldn't think, couldn't do anything but open wider and push back against him, trying to hurry his pace.

He took mercy on me and reached around my hip to brush over my clit until I came apart again, chanting his name.

He pumped into me three more times before losing control and following me over the edge. Hot spurts of his seed filled me, coated me. A second marking. Satisfied for now, he pulled out with a low moan and lay down beside me and pulled me into his arms. I rested my head against his chest and let the cool breeze waft over my bare, tingling skin. With a contented sigh, I reached up and placed my hand against his cheek, nudging him gently until he looked down at me with his spectacular amber eyes.

"You're mine now, Kade. Forever."

He grinned at me. That wolfish grin I loved so dearly. "Yes, Lily. And you're mine."

I came up onto my elbow so I could kiss him with every ounce of love in my heart. He allowed my soft lips to explore him, my hand to wander the curves and planes of his muscled chest, his solid abs…his rock hard cock.

Mating heat rose between us and I smiled as I pushed him onto his back. He'd had his fun. Now it was my turn.

EPILOGUE

ily

"I'm not sure if I can do this," I said.

We stood at the edge of the woods, the sun just starting to set over the line of the trees, the soft haze of summer catching the light. It was beautiful in this forest, so different from the softer hills of Tennessee. I'd never felt at home there as I did in Black Falls, although it had nothing to do with Idaho and everything to do with Kade. He was my home. Where he was, I would be content.

"You can. You just have to trust your wolf," Kade murmured against my neck. He was behind me, his arms wrapped about my waist. I could feel the hard length of him, even the thick ridge of his cock against my lower back. I wiggled my hips, smiled to myself as he groaned. Lowering his head, he nuzzled against the spot he'd bit two weeks ago. There was a small scar there, a true marking, that proved I was a mated female. But I knew every male in Black Falls could scent Kade on me. *I* could scent him. And I loved it, wanted to roll in it, rub myself all over him and wear his favorite t-shirts.

"If you keep rubbing against me like that, we'll never shift."

"Oh?" I asked, smiling, although he couldn't see it. I angled my head to the side so he could have better access to my neck. He knew every place on my body that made me hot. Well, hotter.

I was no longer in heat, but I was always eager for Kade. Maybe it was because I'd been a virgin, but I was insatiable now. I wanted Kade's hands on me, his mouth against my heated skin, his cock deep inside me.

"I can't deny you anything, mate." He bent his knees, slid his cock up against my pussy and then along the seam of my ass. Even through my sundress—he loved me in the pink one I'd worn when he'd first scented me—I felt every ridge, every thick inch of him.

I moaned, wanting more, wanting us naked. I loved him taking me in the forest. Up against a tree, on the soft moss. It was wild and sacred and my wolf almost howled in pleasure. I certainly did.

"Perhaps you can fuck me first, then we can run."

I felt him shake his head, then with hands at my hips, he spun me about.

"You will run first. I will chase you. If I catch you, then we will fuck."

"That doesn't give me a lot of incentive to try very hard," I laughed.

"True." His amber eyes held mine and I saw heat there. He wanted to fuck now. But he'd been trying to get me to shift for over a week and I'd been hesitant. This was the moment. I knew it and he was right, I was stalling. "If I catch you within the first five minutes, you only get one orgasm."

Laughter bubbled up from inside me. Oh, it was *on*. One was not enough. Not nearly enough with my mate, this man who had conquered me body and soul. "If I make it ten minutes, you have to keep your mouth on my pussy until I give you permission to stop."

It was his turn to laugh, his hand buried in my hair. He angled my head to the side and kissed the bite mark on my neck in a pure show of dominance and possession. The move was pure evil. My entire body melted and I wasn't sure I could run five minutes, let alone ten. "Cheater."

"Stop stalling and shift. Be what you were born to be, Lily."

I'd never shifted before, never even knew I was a wolf until just before the claiming. I'd seen him shift, turning from the gorgeous male I loved to a wolf as dark as night. He was big, his back coming to my waist and he looked ruthless, with wicked fangs. But the eyes were the same and I knew it was Kade and he would never hurt me. Only protect me with those strong muscles, vicious teeth.

"What if my wolf is smaller than yours? I won't have a chance," I said on a pout.

He grinned and I watched his teeth lengthen. "I've got news for you, mate, you don't have a chance anyway. I will always catch you. Always."

It was more a vow than a threat and my wolf preened, excited and ready to run. I could feel her about to burst from my skin. I'd been fighting her for a while now, holding her back out of fear. It was time to stop being a coward. And with Kade next to me, I could get through this.

"Okay," I said, sighing. "Let's do this."

He let go of my hips and I stepped back. Once, then again.

I grabbed the hem of my dress and lifted it over my head, letting it fall to the forest floor.

I heard his wolf growl as he took in my naked body. Why should I wear underwear when he only ripped it away?

"So, I should start running?" I asked with a sly grin.

His gaze raked over me, every inch. "Shift, mate. We will run together this time."

"I love you," I said, the words falling from my lips with ease.

Reverence filled his gaze and he stepped closer, cupped my jaw, brushed his knuckles over my nipple.

"My mate. My heart," he said, the words laced with intensity.

He stepped back, dropped his hand. "I see you, Lily. Show me your wolf."

Shifting wasn't about making an effort to change. I realized as I finally let go that it was about surrendering to what I carried inside me. I was wild and powerful, fierce and protective. I let go, stopped holding back, and everything changed in an instant.

It felt like falling, like I'd been spinning in circles until I was so dizzy I had to drop to my knees or fall. I landed on the ground, hard earth and thick leaves under my palms. The vertigo made my head spin and I closed my eyes, afraid I was going to pass out as fire raced through my body like an arc welder tracing every bone.

And then it was over.

Opening my eyes, I thought I smiled, but I couldn't be sure. I looked down to see brown and tan paws. I twisted around and saw the rest of me. I was beautiful, a wild mix of gold and black. Looking around me, I noticed that the colors were dimmed, but I could smell *everything*. And I wanted to run.

Kade dropped to his knees before me and I realized I was looking up at him with a wolf's eyes.

"You're gorgeous, Lily." He reached forward to stroke my

fur and my wolf leaned into his strong hands, eager to be touched, petted, loved. I was so proud of myself, so overflowing with happiness, that a sharp bark left my throat and Kade laughed, his still human eyes sparkling with the same joy I was feeling.

How I had been so lucky, I had no idea. Love filled me up, every empty place, every lonely night I'd ever spent—erased. Kade was mine. He was mine, my mate, and he had a promise to keep.

I might be in a wolf's body, but my mind was working just fine. I looked at my mate's wristwatch, noted the time, and nipped at his wrist with my teeth.

I was already running as Kade yelled at me, pulling his clothes off in a hurry to follow.

Ten minutes. He was so going to pay up.

FIND YOUR MATCH!

YOUR mate is out there. Take the test today and discover your perfect match. Are you ready for a sexy alien mate (or two)?

VOLUNTEER NOW!
interstellarbridesprogram.com

WANT MORE?

Sign up for Grace's VIP Reader list at
http://freescifiromance.com

Read the first chapter of INSERT BOOK TITLE!

Paste here.

Read more now! (Insert link to GG web site)

DO YOU LOVE AUDIOBOOKS?

Grace Goodwin's books are now available as audiobooks…everywhere.

CONNECT WITH GRACE

Interested in joining my not-so-secret Facebook Sci-Fi Squad? Get excerpts, cover reveals and sneak peeks before anyone else. Be part of a closed Facebook group that shares pictures and fun news. JOIN Here: http://bit.ly/SciFiSquad

All of Grace's books can be read as sexy, stand-alone adventures. Her Happily-Ever-Afters are always free from cheating because she writes Alpha males, NOT Alphaholes. (You can figure that one out.) But be careful...she likes her heroes hot and her love scenes hotter. You have been warned...

www.gracegoodwin.com
gracegoodwinauthor@gmail.com

ABOUT GRACE

Grace Goodwin is a *USA Today* and international bestselling author of Sci-Fi & Paranormal romance. Grace believes all women should be treated like princesses, in the bedroom and out of it, and writes love stories where men know how to make their women feel pampered, protected and very well taken care of. Grace hates the snow, loves the mountains (yes, that's a problem) and wishes she could simply download the stories out of her head instead of being forced to type them out. Grace lives in the western US and is a full-time writer, an avid romance reader and an admitted caffeine addict.

ALSO BY GRACE GOODWIN

Interstellar Brides®: Ascension Saga

Ascension Saga, book 1

Ascension Saga, book 2

Ascension Saga, book 3

Trinity: Ascension Saga - Volume 1

Ascension Saga, book 4

Ascension Saga, book 5

Ascension Saga, book 6

Faith: Ascension Saga - Volume 2

Ascension Saga, book 7

Ascension Saga, book 8

Ascension Saga, book 9

Destiny: Ascension Saga - Volume 3

Interstellar Brides® Books

Mastered by Her Mates

Assigned a Mate

Mated to the Warriors

Claimed by Her Mates

Taken by Her Mates

Mated to the Beast

Tamed by the Beast

Mated to the Vikens

Her Mate's Secret Baby

Mating Fever

Her Viken Mates
Fighting For Their Mate
Her Rogue Mates
Claimed By The Vikens

Interstellar Brides®: The Colony
Surrender to the Cyborgs
Mated to the Cyborgs
Cyborg Seduction
Her Cyborg Beast
Cyborg Fever
Rogue Cyborg

Interstellar Brides®: The Virgins
The Alien's Mate
Claiming His Virgin
His Virgin Mate
His Virgin Bride

Other Books
Their Conquered Bride
Wild Wolf Claiming: A Howl's Romance

www.ingramcontent.com/pod-product-compliance
Lightning Source LLC
LaVergne TN
LVHW011852060526
838200LV00054B/4289